Table of Contents

W9-ANO-762

To my father
To Nicole, Conrad and Moneca,
from Toronto to Costa Rica.

1

A Mountain

I love the month of May. The days are
longer, the weather is warmer, and
summer vacation is not far off. The
best thing of all is the Whippy Corners
Agricultural Fair. I am always invited.
If I didn't have to sell chocolate bars,
May would be a perfect month.

But I did have to sell chocolate bars.

I was sitting on my bed, petting my
cat, and thinking dark thoughts. I wasn't
paying attention and I practically
smothered Rick. When Mom came in,
the poor thing was squirming in my
arms and waving his back paws wildly.

Mom cried out, I jumped, and Rick broke free. He fled to the kitchen, shrieking like a band saw.

"Fred!" Mom scolded. "That's no way to treat an animal."

I told her about my worries and I showed her the box of chocolate bars in my closet. Fifty bars, 200 grams each — in other words, a mountain of chocolate!

"Did you have to take so much?" she asked.

I kneaded the cushions, pulled at my comforter, twisted my pillows — anything to avoid admitting my mistake. I had let myself be influenced by my classmates David and Charlie. They had been boasting that they could sell twice as much as that in a single weekend.

Mom grabbed my hands and held them still.

"Stop it, Fred! Calm down! You'll rip that pillow to shreds."

Since I couldn't take it out on inanimate objects, my tension exploded. "I'll never manage to sell it all!"

"Come on, sweetie. It's not the end of the world if you don't."

"It's the end of the world for me! I'll miss my trip because of that chocolate! "

Mom had forgotten the agricultural fair and my weekend at William's. She spread her arms wide.

"Well, all you have to do is sell your chocolate at Whippy Corners!"

What a brilliant idea! I stared at my

mother, but I wasn't seeing her. Instead I saw a spot of light. A ray of sunshine. Something warm and glowing, that would take me in and hold me close.

2
Mud Bath

"Did you know, Fred, that the pig is one of the cleanest creatures in creation?"

Obviously, I didn't believe him, but I played along and looked interested. William's dad loves to tease me, his favourite city-slicker. Every time I visit, he tries to play some trick on me.

Once he told me that you milk cows by pulling on their tail. Another time he claimed that in the winter, cows give ice cream. Now we'd moved on to pigs.

We were standing in front of the pigpen watching the pigs pigging out.

"Their necks are too short, so they can't lick themselves clean. Instead they roll in the mud, and that gets rid of their parasites. Do you know how much your mother would pay for a mud bath?"

I laughed. My mom bathes in water, like everyone else.

Mr. Marshall took a folded magazine from the pocket of his overalls. He opened it and pointed out an advertisement for a beauty spa.

"One hundred and fifty dollars!" he snickered. "To get covered in mud!"

He couldn't stop laughing. I was beginning to think he might be serious this time. After all, the ad was there, in black and white.

"Well, if pigs are so clean, why do we think of them as dirty and messy?"

"Ah!" sighed Mr. Marshall. "People are foolish. They trust only in appearances. Look closely at these pigs, Fred. Don't you think they're cute?"

He gazed at them adoringly. The smallest one must have weighed 135 kilograms, and he was talking as if it was a cute little puppy dog.

Mr. Marshall climbed over the fence and began to scratch the pig's head. Then he pulled on its pink ear and whispered something I couldn't hear.

Surprised, I turned to William. Had his dad lost his mind?

"He's giving the pig instructions. That one's his trotter for the race on Sunday."

I didn't understand. I thought trotters were the pig's feet.

"That one's my dad's best pig," William explained. "His name is Homer. Dad's been training him since last fall. He's certain that pig will win first prize."

"What is the prize? A gold medal?"

"No, a new tractor! Dad really needs one."

"Who's going to ride Homer? Your dad?"

"Oh no! He's way too big. His legs would drag on the ground."

He tapped his chest. "I'm the jockey."

"You never told me!"

"I was afraid you would laugh at me. Aren't you laughing?"

"Do I look like I'm laughing?"

"A little bit…."

In fact, I was having a hard time holding back. Luckily, Mr. Marshall climbed back over the fence and we started walking back to the house.

"Did you know, Fred, that a pig has

forty-four teeth?" he asked.

Forty-four! In my mind, I imagined
Homer with a shark's mouth, full of
teeth. It was too much. I couldn't hold
it any longer. I burst out laughing, so
hard that I slipped and fell on my bum.

Mr. Marshall waved his magazine ad at me.

"Enjoy your mud bath, Fred! This one's on the house!"

3
A Little Snack

The next day, Saturday, we left early for the fair. The first thing Mr. Marshall took us to see was the farm machinery.

After an hour, William and I were exhausted. Our necks ached from looking up at the mechanical monsters. Their tires were twice as tall as we were, and you had to use a stepladder to climb into the driver's seat.

"They're like tanks," I told William.

"Look at this one," he said. "It's for harvesting peas."

"Peas and tank you."

We were so tired that anything we said

sounded funny to us. I should say that we hadn't slept much, because of my cat.

When we visited the pigs, we had left Rick alone in the house. That night he took his revenge.

He spent the whole night running around. Jumping onto the bed, then jumping off. Kneading my stomach. Chasing imaginary mice. And mewing. Scattering his litter on the floor. It was awful!

"Here, guys!" called Mr. Marshall behind us. He handed us two tickets to go on the rides.

"Someone just gave these to me," he explained. "So you use them and have fun while I look at the farm machines some more."

The rides were at the other end of

the fairgrounds. In between were the food stands.

William decided he wanted a little snack. He wolfed down a couple of hot dogs, fries, some fudge, and a stick of cotton candy.

As I watched him, I wondered how

anyone's stomach could hold it. The answer came a half an hour later, when he staggered off the Ferris wheel. It can't.

Poor William. He was pale green and could hardly stand. I managed to borrow a wheelbarrow, loaded him on, and headed back through the binders, the spreaders, and the milkers.

When Mr. Marshall spotted us, he burst out laughing.

We must have looked a sight. I was so hot, my glasses were slipping down my nose. My cap had fallen over my eyes. William was slumped across the wheelbarrow. He looked like a scarecrow that had lost its stuffing.

"Did you win the jackpot, Fred?" Mr. Marshall asked, with a big smile.

Then he realized it was no joke.

William wasn't playing a trick. He was really sick!

"What happened?" he asked.

Queasily, William croaked, "I think I was a bit of a pig."

4
Pinch-Rider

William was asleep on the sofa, cradled by his father, who was staring at the ceiling. He must be thinking about the tractor, which he had absolutely no chance of winning. He hadn't been able to find anyone to ride Homer, now that William was too sick to ride.

The seed of an idea started to sprout in my head.

"What if I tried to ride him, Mr. Marshall?"

"It's very nice of you to offer, Fred, but it wouldn't work. You don't have enough experience, and you might get hurt."

"I've ridden a pony!" I argued.

He managed to keep from laughing. "It's not at all the same."

He was completely against the idea and he wouldn't even let me try to persuade him.

"It's late, kid. Time for bed." He wished me good night, adding, "You'll think differently in the morning."

But the next day I was more determined than ever. I got up at 5:30 and went with Mr. Marshall to the barn. I didn't say anything about riding.

While he was milking the cows, I climbed up to the loft. I was familiar with this spot, as William and I played there every time I visited the farm.

In one corner there was a grain

storage area, with a wall about as high as Homer. On one side there was a thick layer of wheat, and on the other as much hay as anyone could wish for. It was an ideal spot for my training.

I rested an old leather saddle on the wall. I found some old pants and rolled them up, after turning the pockets inside out. That was meant to stand in for Homer's head and his ears. I twisted an old rag up and put it behind the saddle, for the tail. Then I mounted.

I started training with a slow trot. *Ka-clock, ka-clock, ka-clock*. Then I went to a faster trot. *Tack-tack-tack-tack*. Then a gallop: *tacketa-tacketa-tacketa*.

Boom. I toppled over onto the grain. I picked myself up, dusted myself off,

and got back on the saddle.

Suddenly I noticed Mr. Marshall watching me, chewing on a blade of hay.

"Having lots of fun, I see."

"I'm not fooling around. I'm training!"

He frowned. I could tell he still disagreed with my plan. But this time he let me speak, and I managed to persuade him.

"Just one condition," he said.

"What?"

"You have to wear a helmet, knee pads, elbow pads, and wrist guards."

"I'll look like a total idiot!"

"You either wear them or you don't ride. I can't risk you getting hurt."

I grumbled a bit, but how could I

hope to win the race if I wasn't in the running? So I agreed. If I wound up looking like an idiot, so be it.

5

A Tortoise on the Back of a Pig

William was in bed still when I went back to the house. He was almost as pale as the evening before. He couldn't swallow a thing. He said he still felt too queasy. I brought Rick over to comfort him. William smiled at him weakly.

I sat down on the bed and told him my plan.

"You'd really do that for me?"

"For you and your dad. After all, you brought me the cat of my dreams!"

"Aren't you afraid you'll fall off?"

"Your dad's making me wear a

helmet, knee pads, elbow pads, and
wrist guards."

"Bummer! You'll look like — "

" — like a tortoise on the back of a
pig. I know!"

Mr. Marshall came up when he
heard us laughing. He was happy to see
a little colour in William's cheeks, and
gave him a big hug.

I don't know why, but it made me
think of the sun coming out after the

rain. I said to myself, *May really is the best month of the year!*

Then, suddenly, I remembered the chocolate. Darn, I'd forgotten all about it! It was already noon on Sunday and I hadn't sold a single bar!

I told William and his dad I had to get ready for the race. I had just realized what a pickle I had gotten myself into.

I had two options. I could sell chocolate to help my class, or I could ride the pig to help William and his father.

What should I do?

I needed energy to think. I grabbed a chocolate bar and went out. I decided to visit the pigs. Maybe when I saw them the answer to my problem would come to me.

Homer had been scrubbed and pampered. Mr. Marshall had washed him and put him in a private sty, with fresh straw. He *was* an awfully cute pig. He came over to me, sniffing.

It seems pigs have a really good sense of smell. By the time I remembered that, the chocolate bar I was holding had disappeared in one gulp down Homer's gullet. What a pig! He hadn't even chewed it! And he was still sniffing my hand.

A bit annoyed, I turned away and was about to go back to the house when I had an idea. I ran to find Mr. Marshall.

"If I win the tractor for you, will you buy my chocolate off me?"

"That would not be a lot to pay for a new tractor, Fred," he laughed. "You're not much of a businessman!"

"Well?" I asked impatiently. "Yes or no?"

"What if you don't win?"

"I'll win."

"That's what I like — a kid with confidence!" he exclaimed, clapping me on the back. "You've got the stuff of a champion!"

And he shook my hand so hard I wondered if I'd be strong enough to ride. But it wasn't my strength that would win the race. It was Homer's speed. And I knew how to get that!

6

A Firecracker Tied to His Tail

Mom had told me a hundred times: sugar is a stimulant. Eating too much candy would make me hyper. The only way to calm down was to run until I was exhausted. Otherwise, I would never fall asleep.

Homer gobbled down the chocolate bars as fast as I could unwrap them. What a rocket he'd be once he'd started to digest them! All I would have to do is hold on tight and the race would be won. I would be crowned champion, and Mr. Marshall would have a new tractor!

It was nearly time to leave. Mr. Marshall was pulling up the truck to load Homer.

Stuffed to the gills, Homer was sprawled in a corner of his sty. He wouldn't budge. Mr. Marshall tied a leash around his neck and pulled, but nothing doing. Homer was stuck.

Mr. Marshall scratched his head. He'd never seen his best racer in such a sluggish state.

At his wits' end, he poked Homer in the behind with a pitchfork. What else could he do?

Homer leapt up. He acted like he was trying to tear off a firecracker tied to his tail. He spun around like a top.

William had found just enough energy to come with us to the fair. He

sat in the truck holding Rick and
laughing his head off. He'd never seen
anything so funny, he told us.

I wasn't laughing so hard.

I imagined myself sitting on the back of that spinning top. Had I gone too far? Fortunately, Homer finally calmed down a bit. He collapsed onto his bed of straw, fell asleep, and started snoring.

"What's with this pig?" exclaimed Mr. Marshall, exasperated.

He pulled out the hose and sprayed Homer with cold water. Homer tottered to his feet and shook himself off.

"Hallelujah!" cried Mr. Marshall joyfully.

He clapped me on the back.

"Do you realize, Fred, what would have happened if Homer here had let us down? You would have had to spend the afternoon selling chocolate bars!"

7

Hard to Miss

The racers were lined up at the starting
line. There were about twenty of us,
all about the same age and the same
size. The riders all looked alike and the
pigs all looked alike.

Except for Homer and me. I stood
out because I was the only one wearing
a helmet and pads. Homer was hard to
miss because he was the only pig lying
on its back with its hooves in the air.

The spectators were rolling in the
aisles, Mr. Marshall was tearing his
hair out, and William was looking
perplexed. I felt ashamed and

desperate. How would I get out of this mess?

The starting pistol went off. The riders climbed onto their mounts and galloped off.

They were already far off in the distance when I managed, by jerking on his leash, to get Homer to his feet.

I jumped onto his back and pressed my heels into his flanks to get him going. He moved not an inch.

Then, when I was least expecting it, Homer reared up on his back feet. He performed a little dance like Zorro's horse, then sprang forward like a comet!

I grabbed onto him wherever I could — his leash, his neck, his ears — to keep from falling. The crowd was screaming with laughter. Homer seemed to be spurred on by the noise, and he hurtled after the other racers. In a few moments, we had caught up to them.

Homer galloped on at a breakneck pace. We squeezed between the other pigs and then we were ahead of them, at the front of the pack. The commentator was yelling into the microphone.

"What a sprint, ladies and gentlemen! What a terrific trio!"

Trio? What was he talking about?

"Nothing like this has ever been seen before in Whippy Corners! Tandem piggyback riders!"

Tandem …? I had heard that word before. Didn't it mean *two?* I was puzzled, but I couldn't waste time on it because Homer was giving me too much to think about. The finish line was coming up and I couldn't figure out how to slow him down.

Suddenly, the announcer's words clicked in my brain and everything became clear. I swiveled my head and there was my cat, hanging on to Homer's tail for dear life.

It was Rick's claws that had made Homer take off and run, not my kicks in the flanks or my great skill as a rider!

Poor kitty! He had only wanted to help me. He didn't know what he was getting himself into. I had to rescue him.

I did the only thing I could. I wriggled around on the pig until I was facing the riders behind me. Now I had my back to the finish line.

I squeezed Homer's flanks to stay on and laid across his back. I stretched out my arms to grab Rick and pulled. It was like pulling a burr off a woolen sock.

Once Rick's claws were out of him, Homer came to an abrupt halt. My

legs loosened their grip and I
catapulted backwards through the air
to the finish line.

Homer stood stock still in the

middle of the track. He watched the other racers go by, looking as if he wondered where the fire was.

I had no time to get out of the way. Flat on my face, I watched them gallop near me in a thick cloud of dust.

I thought about the tractor that I had almost won. I thought about William and his father and how worried they must be. I thought about my parents, and my little brother, and my grandmother, and how sad they would be.

I thought about all the chocolate I had wasted. And Homer, who would surely be sick to his stomach. And Rick, who seemed to have disappeared.

Then everything went black, and I told myself that I must be dead.

8
Pigsty Perfume

I could hear voices. I could see cat fur.
It sure was strange in heaven. It
smelled like a pigsty.

"Don't touch him until the
ambulance arrives," someone said.

"If we could at least get that cat off his
face," a woman answered. "Shoo! Shoo!"

"Leave it alone. Can't you see it's
frightened?"

"It's weird, a cat lying on his helmet
like that. It looks like he's wearing a
fur hat!"

"Wait! I'll take care of it. Rick, come
here. Here, kitty. Don't be afraid. It's

me, William. Do you recognize me?"

My head suddenly felt lighter, and I wasn't surrounded by blackness. I could see dirt. I blinked my eyes behind my scratched lenses.

"Look, he moved! Fred! Can you hear me?"

"I can't hear you. I'm dead."

"What are you talking about? If you were dead, you wouldn't be talking!"

"That's true. Maybe I was dead before, but I'm not anymore. Before, everything was black."

"That's because your cat's tail was draped over your eyes. Look! I'm holding Rick now."

I cautiously raised my head. No pain. I stood up, moved my arms and legs around.

"Everything working?" An ambulance attendant pushed through the crowd.

"Working just fine!"

"Whew!" sighed William and his dad. "We were worried about you!"

But I was worried about Homer.

"Where is he? I don't see him."

"He was taken to the veterinarian."

"Really? How come?"

"Oh my! A lot of things happened, there, while you were dead."

After throwing me off, Homer had gotten up and won the race. He had streaked forward like an arrow from a bow, and crossed the finish line half a

metre ahead of the others.

"Then," said William, "he got sick. He threw up in front of everybody. I wonder what he could have eaten!"

"The judges are wondering too," he added in a whisper. "Homer's behaviour was very strange. He was like a racecar backfiring."

"What does that have to do with the judges?"

"Sometimes athletes are disqualified, like in the Olympics, because they've taken illegal substances."

"Do you think Homer might be disqualified?"

"That depends on what the vet says."

Suddenly, everything seemed to spin and grow blurry. William's voice seemed to be coming from far away.

"Watch out! He's going to fall," shouted the ambulance attendant.

He caught me just in time. Afterwards, everything turned black again, and it wasn't because of cat fur. Rick was still in William's arms. I know, because that was the last thing I saw before I fainted.

9
Confession

I thought of Homer as I lay on the stretcher. I prayed that Mr. Marshall would keep his pig. He was sitting beside me in the ambulance — Mr. Marshall, that is, not the pig. I couldn't keep from shedding a tear or two.

Mr. Marshall grabbed my hand and patted it.

"What's up, Fred? Why are you crying?"

"Can a pig die of an upset stomach?"

"I'd be surprised. And never Homer! He might lose a kilogram or two, but he'd gain them right back — he's such a glutton."

I swallowed my sobs and sighed, "Tell me about it."

"What do you mean?"

I closed my eyes and took a deep breath. It's not always easy to tell the truth. But I gathered my courage and jumped in, my voice quavering a little.

"I thought I was doing the right thing."

Mr. Marshall stroked my hair. "You did fine, Fred. You won the race! Homer won't be disqualified, I can guarantee that. He didn't ingest anything illegal."

"Is chocolate illegal?"

"No. Why do you ask?"

"I gave him chocolate."

"Lots?"

"Lots and lots."

"How much?"

"The whole box."

Mr. Marshall thought about this in silence. He must have been so angry! After a few seconds, he said, "With his weight, that might not be as much as it seems. Let me see."

He took out his calculator and started punching numbers in.

"Relatively speaking, it's as if you had eaten …"

He pressed a button and gaped at the machine. "One-point-two-five kilograms!"

I felt sick just thinking about it. Poor Homer!

"Now I understand why he had so much energy," said Mr. Marshall. "But I don't understand the backfiring …"

"Could that have been the paper?"

"What!? Did you give him the paper too?"

"No, of course not, Mr. Marshall," I answered, offended. "He stole it when my back was turned."

10
A Good Lesson

Nothing was broken and there were no hidden injuries, so the doctor sent me home.

Half an hour later, the vet arrived with Homer. He had signed a document saying that, aside from certain mild digestive problems, the pig was perfectly normal. He could keep his championship.

"Hooray, Dad!" cried William. "We won the tractor!"

"Yep," Mr. Marshall replied.

I could tell he was pleased, but that didn't keep him from adding, "It could have turned out very badly and I think you both need to be punished for your recklessness."

I protested. I was the only one who had stuffed Homer with chocolate. I didn't want William to have to take any blame.

"I remind you, Fred, that if William had not stuffed himself, none of this would have happened. For your punishment, the two of you will clean out Homer's sty after dinner."

Was that all? We were relieved. I ate heartily, and so did William, although he was still feeling a bit iffy.

Afterwards, we put on our overalls and went out to Homer's pen. We had no idea what was awaiting us there. Talk about a pigsty! There was filth

everywhere. It would take us hours to clean it up.

"I think I'm going to be sick," said William.

"No way!" I cried. "We've got work to do!"

We were still wondering where to start when we heard a familiar sound. Mr. Marshall drove up on his tractor. He stopped beside the pigpen.

"How's it going, guys? Making progress?"

"Ye-e-e-es," William answered unenthusiastically.

"I was going to offer to give you a hand, but since you don't need me ..."

And he drove off. I glared at William.

"Couldn't you have kept quiet?"

With the tractor, his dad would have finished the job in fifteen minutes, while we would be there with our shovels for hours!

William looked down and mumbled, "Sometimes it's hard to tell the truth."

"I know," I replied. "But it's always worth it!"

We dropped our shovels and ran after Mr. Marshall and his tractor.

He was kind. He helped us clean up the pigpen, and afterwards offered to make us a snack. I almost asked for hot chocolate, but I stopped myself. I didn't want to seem like a pig!

Fred and the Pig Race

Fred and the Pig Race

Marie-Danielle Croteau

Illustrated by Bruno St-Aubin
Translated by Sarah Cummins

First Novels

Formac Publishing Company Limited
Halifax, Nova Scotia

Originally published as *Été du cochon*
Copyright © 2006 Les éditions de la courte échelle inc.
Translation copyright © 2007 Sarah Cummins

Formac Publishing Company Limited recognizes the support of the
Province of Nova Scotia through the Department of Tourism, Culture and
Heritage. We acknowledge the financial support of the Government of
Canada through the Book Publishing Industry Development Program
(BPIDP) for our publishing activities.

Formac Publishing Company Limited acknowledges the support of the
Canada Council for the Arts for our publishing program.

Library and Archives Canada Cataloguing in Publication

Croteau, Marie-Danielle, 1953-
[Été du cochon. English]
   Fred and the pig race / Marie-Danielle Croteau ; illustrated by Bruno
St-Aubin ; translated by Sarah Cummins.

(First novels ; #61)
Translation of: L'été du cochon.
ISBN 978-0-88780-733-6 (bound).--ISBN 978-0-88780-731-2 (pbk.)

   1. Swine--Juvenile fiction. I. St-Aubin, Bruno II. Cummins, Sarah
III. Title. IV. Title: Été du cochon. English . V. Series.

PS8555.R6185E8413 2007   jC843'.54   C2007-904109-4

Formac Publishing Company Ltd.
5502 Atlantic Street
Halifax, Nova Scotia, B3H 1G4
www.formac.ca

Printed and bound in Canada